D0100183

A Note to Parents

Eyewitness Readers is a compelling new program
for beginning readers, designed in conjunction with
leading literacy experts, including Dr. Linda Gambrell,
President of the National Reading Conference and past
board member of the International Reading Association.

Eyewitness has become the most trusted name in
illustrated books, and this new series combines the highly
visual *Eyewitness* approach with engaging, easy-to-read
stories. Each *Eyewitness Reader* is guaranteed to
capture a child's interest while developing his or her
reading skills, general knowledge, and love of reading.

The four levels of *Eyewitness Readers* are aimed
at different reading abilities, enabling you to choose
the books that are exactly right for your children:

Level 1, for **Preschool to Grade 1**
Level 2, for **Grades 1 to 3**
Level 3, for **Grades 2 and 3**
Level 4, for **Grades 2 to 4**

The "normal" age at which a child
begins to read can be anywhere
from three to eight years old,
so these levels are intended
only as a general guideline.

No matter which level
you select, you can be sure
that you are helping
your child learn to read,
then read to learn!

A DK PUBLISHING BOOK
www.dk.com

Editor Dawn Sirett
Art Editor Jane Horne

Senior Editor Linda Esposito
Senior Art Editor Diane Thistlethwaite
US Editor Regina Kahney
Production Melanie Dowland
Picture Researcher Angela Anderson
Jacket Designer Chris Drew
Natural History Consultant
Theresa Greenaway

Reading Consultant
Linda B. Gambrell, Ph.D.

First American Edition, 2000
2 4 6 8 10 9 7 5 3 1
Published in the United States by DK Publishing, Inc.
95 Madison Avenue, New York, New York 10016

Copyright © 2000 Dorling Kindersley Limited, London
All rights reserved under International and Pan-American Copyright
Conventions. No part of this publication may be reproduced, stored
in a retrieval system, or transmitted in any form or by any means,
electronic, mechanical, photocopying, recording, or otherwise,
without the prior written permission of the copyright owner.

Published in Great Britain by Dorling Kindersley Limited.

Eyewitness Readers™ is a trademark of Dorling Kindersley Limited, London.

Library of Congress Cataloging-in-Publication Data

Wallace, Karen.
  Wild baby animals / by Karen Wallace. -- 1st American ed.
  p. cm. -- (Eyewitness readers. Level 1)
  Summary: Describes some of the differences in the ways various baby animals--
including monkeys, rhinos, wolves, seals, and elephants--behave and grow.
  ISBN 0-7894-5420-3 (hardcover) -- ISBN 0-7894-5419-X (pbk.)
  1. Animals--Infancy--Juvenile literature. [1. Animals--Infancy.]
I. Title. II. Series.

QL763.D74 2000
591.3'9 21--dc21   99-043586

Color reproduction by Colourscan, Singapore
Printed and bound in Belgium by Proost

The publisher would like to thank the following for
their kind permission to reproduce their photographs:
Key: a=above, c=center, b=below, l=left, r=right, t=top
Ardea London Ltd: Peter Steyn 4 bl; **Bruce Coleman Collection Ltd:**
Trevor Barrett 6–7, 19 c, Erwin & Peggy Bauer 28, Fred Bruemmer 10 t,
Alain Compost front cover, 17, Peter Davey 26 b, Chrisler Fredriksson 27 cl,
32 crb, Janos Jurka 22 t, Steven C. Kaufman 15 t, 15 cr, 32 bl, Gunter Kohler
16 c, Stephen Krasemann 24 b, Leonard Lee 7 t, Joe McDonald 3 b, 23 b,
M. R. Phicton 4 cra, 4 cr, Jorg & Petra Wegner 5 b; **NHPA:** B. & C. Alexander
12 b; **Oxford Scientific Films:** Martyn Colbeck 9 t, 30–31 b, Daniel J. Cox
14 tr, 14–15 b, Kenneth Day 5 tr, 13 t, 32 tl, Michael Fogden 13 b,
Zig Leszczynski 10 b; **Planet Earth Pictures:** Gary Bell 29 c, 29 inset, 32 br,
Tom Brakefield 21 t, Robert Franz 25, M. & C. Denis Huot 2 br, 18 b,
Brian Kenney 27 t, Pavlo de Oliveira 8–9 b, Doug Perrine 20–21 b.

Additional photography for DK:
Peter Anderson, Jane Burton, Frank Greenaway,
Colin Keates, Dave King, Bill Ling, and Tim Ridley.

FREETOWN SCHOOL
MEDIA CENTER

DK EYEWITNESS READERS

BEGINNING
1
TO READ

Wild
Baby Animals

Written by Karen Wallace

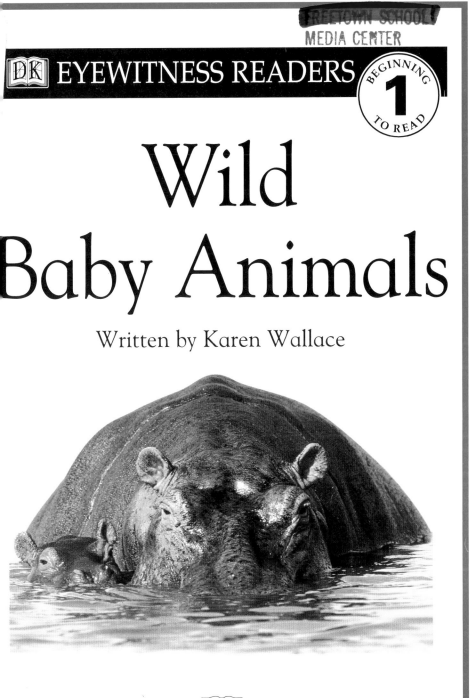

DK
DK PUBLISHING, INC.

Animals grow up in different ways
They have lots of lessons to learn.
Some are born helpless,
but their mothers protect them.

A newborn kangaroo is the size
of a bee.

She crawls
into her
mother's
safe pouch.

She doesn't open
her eyes for at least
five months.

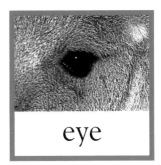

eye

A newborn monkey cannot walk.
He is carried by his mother.

Other baby animals
can walk soon after they're born.
They learn to run
with their mother
when danger is near.

Baby rhinos stand on their hooves
a few minutes after
they are born.

hooves

A baby zebra can run
an hour after she is born.

Some baby animals are born
in a place that is safe.
Other baby animals are born
in the open.

Baby wolves are born in a cave.

A baby elephant is born
on open, grassy land.

Other elephants
make a circle
to protect her.

All the animals in this book
drink their mother's milk.
They are called mammals.

A seal's milk is fatty and rich.
Baby seals need lots of fat
to keep warm in the snow.

Baby bears
suck milk
for six months.

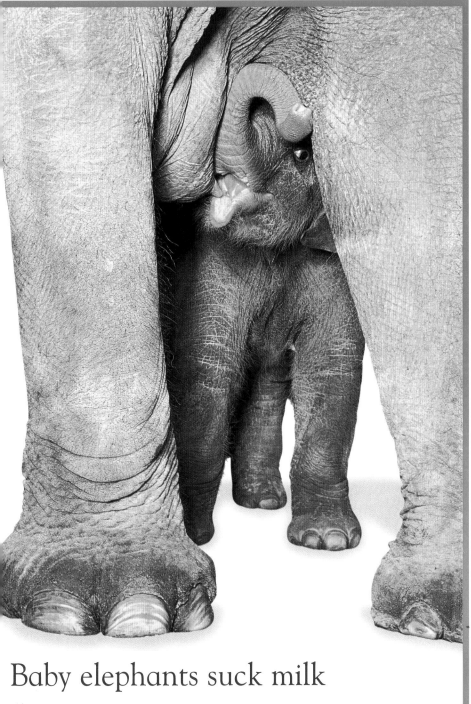

Baby elephants suck milk
for two years or more!

All baby mammals
stay by their mother
to keep safe.

On land, a baby walrus
stays tucked under her mother.

A baby kangaroo is carried
in his mother's pouch.

A baby sloth has to hold on tight.
Her mother is upside down!

Baby animals
must stay clean
to be healthy.

tongue

A mother cheetah
licks her cub's soft fur
with her rough tongue.

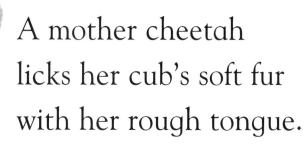

A monkey picks lice
from her baby's back
with her long fingers.

fingers

As baby animals grow
they need solid food.

Lion cubs eat
what their mother can catch.

Baby orangutans
eat fruit
that their mother
has chewed for them.

Other baby animals
soon find food for themselves.

A baby buffalo
eats grass.

lips

A baby giraffe tears off leaves
with her thick lips.

Baby animals
know their mother's voice.
They find her quickly
if danger is near.

A baby dolphin
hears her mother
make a click-click-click sound.

CLICK!

CLICK!

CLICK!

A baby seal
knows her mother's bark. ARRK!

When there's danger in the water, baby animals do as they're told.

Baby beavers dive when they hear the whack of their mother's tail.

tail

A baby hippo
stays with his mother
when she grunts a loud warning.

When there's danger
in the forest,
baby animals do as they're told.

A fawn lies still
in the grass
so she won't be seen.

Bear cubs
climb a tree
when their
mother growls.

As baby animals grow older
they start
to look after themselves.

A young chimpanzee
uses a stick to dig for insects.

Otter cubs learn to swim
so they can
catch fish.

trunk

A young elephant
uses her trunk
to rip leaves
from a tree.

Baby animals play games
that teach them how
to look after themselves.

Wolf cubs wrestle and bite.
They're pretending to hunt.

Baby koalas play in the trees.
They're learning to climb
with their sharp claws.

claws

Baby animals grow up.
They learn their lessons well
and no longer need
their mothers.

Koalas are
fully grown
at two years.

Elephants are
fully grown
at twenty-five!

One day baby animals
are old enough
to have babies of their own.

Picture Word List

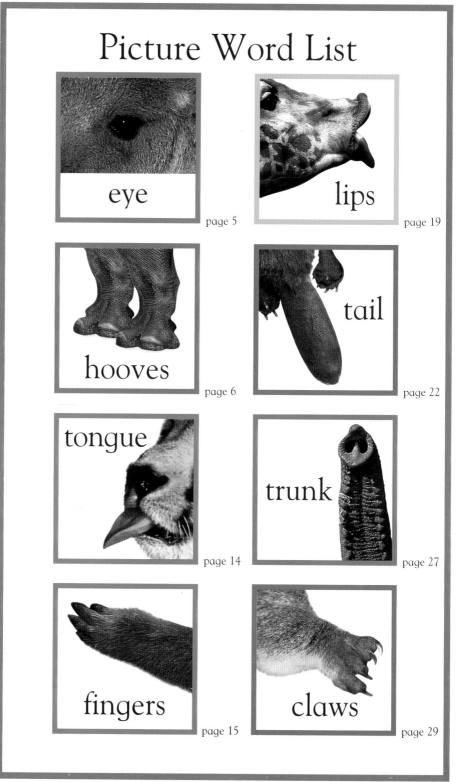

eye
page 5

lips
page 19

hooves
page 6

tail
page 22

tongue
page 14

trunk
page 27

fingers
page 15

claws
page 29

[DK] EYEWITNESS READERS

Level 1
Beginning to Read

A Day at Greenhill Farm
Truck Trouble
Tale of a Tadpole
Surprise Puppy!
Duckling Days
A Day at Seagull Beach
Whatever the Weather
Busy Buzzy Bee
Big Machines
Wild Baby Animals
Lego: Trouble at the Bridge

Level 2
Beginning to Read Alone

Dinosaur Dinners
Fire Fighter!
Bugs! Bugs! Bugs!
Slinky, Scaly Snakes!
Animal Hospital
The Little Ballerina
Munching, Crunching, Sniffing,
    and Snooping
The Secret Life of Trees
Winking, Blinking, Wiggling,
    and Waggling
Astronaut – Living in Space
Lego: Castle Under Attack!

Level 3
Reading Alone

Spacebusters
Beastly Tales
Shark Attack!
Titanic
Invaders from Outer Space
Movie Magic
Plants Bite Back!
Time Traveler
Bermuda Triangle
Tiger Tales
Aladdin
Heidi
Lego: Mission to the Arctic

Level 4
Proficient Readers

Days of the Knights
Volcanoes
Secrets of the Mummies
Pirates!
Horse Heroes
Trojan Horse
Micromonsters
Going for Gold!
Extreme Machines
Flying Ace – The Story of
    Amelia Earhart
Robin Hood
Black Beauty
Lego: Race for Survival